GOD'S GREATEST MIRACLE

A TALE OF TWO LITTLE ANGELS

(A Love Story Christ Gifted to Miriam and His Beloved Disciple)

JEAN-MICHEL POLYAKOV

Founding Pastor, Church of Christs Christianity

tellwell

Tellwell Talent
www.tellwell.ca

ISBN
978-0-2288-5689-4 (Hardcover)
978-0-2288-5688-7 (Paperback)
978-0-2288-5690-0 (eBook)

Reviews for God's Greatest Miracle

1

In the spirit of the Oral Tradition and reminiscent of the Bards of times past, **God's Greatest Miracle: A Tale of Two Little Angels** captures universal wisdom common to several faiths. It presents it in a storytelling manner easy for both the young and the old to understand.

The book's few pages are rich with teachings presented in a story that readers will long remember. A tale integrating Eastern and Western wisdom masterfully and so touching the heart. Who better conveys a vital teaching of the New Testament, the need to be as little children to enter the Kingdom of Heaven, than the protagonists that the author has chosen? But the book does much more. It introduces the concepts of reincarnation, reintegration with one's Divine Nature, right living, and the need to listen to the still small voice within. To live our lives actionably and consciously. Even onto assuming the role of Bodhisattvas. For multiple reasons, this little treasure chest offers a ray of hope in today's turbulent times.

Personally, this book reinforced my sense of Divine Protection, even though I do not regard myself as a Prince or a Chosen One. Because of the book's uplifting and enlightening messages, I will be re-reading it from time to time. I recommend it to other students on the Path of our return to the Source.

God's Greatest Miracle is an easy read, and its brevity is one of its many strengths. It is a teaching tale that needs sharing universally across the world's great faiths. And yes, it is true for everyone, both young and old! **David Stein, PhD, Founding Editor-in-Chief, FUTUREtakes, Nevada: Rating 5 Stars**

2

God's Greatest Miracle: A Tale of Two Little Angels (A Teaching Tale for Everyone, Young or Old) by Jean-Michel Polyakov,

Baron du Mont Saint Germain, is the first codex in the Nouseum Sagas. This children's tale is a story within a story. A traveller is transported to an unknown country that seems free from poverty, sickness, and greed. An old man speaks to the traveller and tells him his heart has brought him to this place. He is introduced to the beloved Prince and Princess of the country and then given an important task: to tell the world about God's Greatest Miracle: A Tale of Two Little Angels.

This is a children's story that directs readers to look into their innermost selves. The traveller is invited to the beautiful Grand City in Nouseum, named after the city's inherent Nature. While there, he learns many things. Meeting the eyes of the Prince, he experiences the pain of the world, and when he meets the Princess's eyes, he experiences peace and joy. In this part of the tale, I could genuinely feel the traveller's enlightenment as he prays to the Guardian, Messenger of True Conscience.

My interest in the story was piqued when the traveller is asked to share an incredible teaching tale. God's Greatest Miracle: A Tale of Two Little Angels by Jean-Michel Polyakov, Baron du Mont Saint Germain enriches the heart and the mind with lessons we have either forgotten or have yet to learn. It is well-paced and gives off a sincere aura; you can tell from the story that this was a labour of love. This tale teaches us the importance of loving each other, standing up for what you believe in, and it also encourages the pursuit of knowledge. It is a privilege to have read such a touching tale of love and hope. **Reviewed By Jessica Barbosa for Readers' Favorite Reviews: Rating 4 Stars**

3

Jean-Michel Polyakov is a gifted writer. His writing style flows effortlessly through this extraordinary tale. I found myself pulled into the story, bringing a smile from within. The story reinforces the importance of working to become the best you can be. Those who read this teaching tale will want to make a positive difference in this world and the world to come. Yes, love overcomes darkness. God's Greatest Miracle is delightful reading for all ages. **Dr Ray DuRussel, Physician, Texas: Rating 5 Stars**

4

Finding and reading this little Christian fairy tale is like rubbing a lamp and having a Djinn flow out of the spout with a Wish. You open and begin reading this book, and your heart fills with the Unconditional Love God placed in the Author's heart to share with his readers. You wonder how can such an immense treasure be in such a small vessel. But then you remember Yeshua's fondness for children born from out of the Kingdom of Heaven Within. I recommend **God's Greatest Miracle. A Tale of Two Little Angels** to everyone, but especially to Christians who actively help God. **Andrew David, thephoenixmentor, Florida: Rating 5 Stars**

5

Baron Jean-Michel aptly weaves together a touching tale of Heaven and Earth to share the story of two angel children, a boy and a girl. The tale deftly blends religion, metaphysics, and spiritual elements. Even the Archangels take a serious interest in the two. We glimpse the Celestial workings, the necessity of stewardship, and the power of love—a profound and worthwhile read. **Jeanne Marie Dunworth, Clinical Psychotherapist, Maryland: Rating 5 Stars**

6

God's Greatest Miracle is a timely story about the battle between good and evil individually and within humanity: we all need a reminder to choose the high road, especially during difficult times. Reading this little book will bring some moments of simple joy into your life. Perhaps you will learn to love more fully? I enjoyed it immensely, even with British English. **Dr Laura Temin, Marital and Family Therapist, Georgia: Rating 4 Stars**

7

Though English isn't my first language, I found the book easy to read and connect with. I hope that this timely tale comes true for our world. Americans may not fully appreciate the wisdom and love placed into this story. However, having experienced totalitarianism personally in the USSR, I understand the gifts of freedom, human kindness, and love. **Eteri Yarovsky, Nurse, Georgia: Rating 5 Stars**

8

An age-old answer is whether we are born good or bad. The Author addresses this question in his pleasant and engaging story of two little angels. Most say that we are born in a neutral position. However, our lifetime of experiences dictates our purpose in life, ethics, and morals.

The Author offers another theory of the development of our ethics and character. By pleasantly taking us through a simple child-like story, he presents a new approach to our ultimate Nature and the development of our essences.

In today's world of digitising communication and politicising, this vessel of spiritual guidance provides a more meaningful approach to life's challenges. It returns us to a comfortable thought process of who we are and what we want to become.

What I found most interesting is the Author's approach to the concept of the human soul. When is it formed, how does it develop, and where it goes after leaving this Heavenly God created planet?

I recommend this tome wholeheartedly to those pondering their lives. **Frank J Klosik Jr Attorney at Law (Emeritus), South Carolina: Rating 5 Stars**

9

I recommend Jean-Michel's story about two little angels making unconditional love a reality. I wish we could do this, for I see so much oppression and unkindness around me. My little ones speak Ukrainian, so I could not read it to them, but retold the story so they would understand. My little girl told me she wants to be an angel and help people love each other. This story is powerfully strong in love and caring. Only an absolute angel could have written it. The altruism and spiritual lessons taught in this small book will impress the young and the elderly. I admire the Author of this book. He was really born to make this world better. Changing our world is up to each of us. Here and there. **Julia Klimenko, Translator, Poltava, Ukraine: Rating 5 Stars**

10

I am a voracious reader, but I must admit that I have not come across a more touching and enlightening tale than that written by Jean-Michel Polyakov. **God's Greatest Miracle. A Tale of Two Little Angels** (A Love Story Gifted by Christ to Miriam and His Beloved Disciple).

As I read this sweet story, I experienced tears of sorrow and tears of deep happiness. By the end of the book, my hope in the possibility of our species finally becoming what God wishes us to be was renewed. Reading this tale will bring your heart closer to God.

The storyline of this short tome is how two special angels find each other after incarnating, fall in love, and manifest a true miracle on earth by listening to God.

Every church Pastor in English-speaking countries should buy this book and convert it into a sermon on the power of real love and perseverance. I recommend it to Christians of all denominations (and everyone else with a good heart).

Perhaps Jean-Michel's book is another miracle inspired by God. **Christopher Sagen, Monterey Bay Aquarium Facilities Systems Manager, retired. Universal Life Church Minister 5: Rating 5 Stars**

11

This little book teaches us to go back to the place of unconditional love that we were born into. Follow the little angels as they take us through that journey to a beautiful home we can revisit to thrive in life. We never lost this in childhood, so this is just a journey back to that splendid time for all of us, with the wisdom of Jean-Michel as our guide. **God's Greatest Miracle** is a must-read for the family. **Tacy Trump, Senior Executive Producer, VoiceAmerica, WorldTalkRadio, LLC: Rating 5 Stars**

12

Jean-Michel presents the reading public with a true masterpiece of spirituality. **God's Greatest Miracle. A Tale of Two Little Angels** reminding us that human love should be as close to unconditional as possible. His teaching tale is about moving from our world of egoism and greed into the Kingdom of Heaven on Earth or the mythical Golden Age of humankind.

In the book, we discover two baby angels who were firstborn in Heaven. They came into the physical, found each other, dedicated their lives to healthcare, and overcame oppression and poverty. The book has a great ending, as you will find out if you read it.

Lady Kiara Warwick, Genealogist, England: Rating 5 Stars.

13

All books worth reading encourage a reader to explore their life. Further, it takes natural talent with a pen to write a fictional work that captures our reality. Jean-Michel is a talented author fascinated with exploring who God is. Using fiction is a brilliant method for the author to help us understand why a life spent in altruism and charity is well-lived. Everyone has a worldview. Still, God is who God is. God has a purpose for each of us in fulfilling God's Plan, and it requires love.

The beauty of this book is that it reminds us that no one knows all that there is to know about God and His love. Loving as Jesus did helps us understand God better. This book shows the importance of allowing God's Kingdom to rule us in our specific circumstances and correct our understanding. While this teaching tale does not provide facts about God or finding God, we see the author's point. God is busy revealing himself to us right where we are through angelic activity, Jesus, and the events of our daily lives. **Pastor**

Brian Downing, Oakdale Church of God, Georgia: Rating 5 Stars

14

Some days, I feel like a boulder resting firm in a robust mountain stream. There I sit, as the water of time flows past, carrying so many unconscious creatures to oblivion. Early this morning, Father Sun rose from his nocturnal rest with Mother Night to light my vision. Trapped in front of me, spinning in a wee swirl of the River of Time, turned a small tome. I reached down to retrieve it from temporality. It wasn't large, but it took much effort to lift it. Clearly, the message it contained was substantial. On its cover was a small footbridge passing over a bit of stream in a secluded forest. I know this place from Narnia.

The tome contained a wondrous tale of two little angels who loved each other so much that the world they came to live within was filled with God's Love. It is titled appropriately: God's Greatest Miracle. A Tale to Two Little Angels.

The writing is superb, and the story flows well. Only a hard-hearted person would miss the love placed into this tale by the Author.

When I began to read, I left my boulder and became the little boy angel. His dear heart was filled with as much love as was the Lord's. Reading further, I knew this story was a new chapter in the Holy Books. Indeed, the boy and girl angels are married before God and came to their Earth as God's helpers.

As I lived the story, the Lord's message about the Kingdom of Heaven on Earth didn't seem so far away if we turn towards God and not the Deceiver.

I look forward to speaking with Baron Polyakov when he travels to Narnia next time. Aslan wants to meet him. Delivered by an angel. **CS Lewis, Christian Author, Narnia: Rating 5 Iridescent Stars radiating Wisdom and Love to all**

Request for Post-Launch Reviews

Amazon-Kindle is the major bookseller globally (print, eBook, and audiobooks). Moreover, an Author's success depends upon readers understanding Amazon-Kindle's marketing stipulations. For example, Amazon-Kindle wants readers to provide short reviews for placement on the book page. If readers do not post reviews, Amazon-Kindle will penalise the Author and book sales suffer even for a great read.

So, I ask you to place a short review telling why you like this book. A review of one to ten lines is sufficient. Amazon would like sixty or more views.

The monies generated belong to our Church and cover education outreach and medical research.

Bless all of you—God speed.

Jean-Michel

Dedication

I dedicate this book to several courageous nuns ministering in Puerto Rico in the early 1950s. Firstly, to Sister Anna Marie who loved and cared for me like a mother and died young from consumption. Secondly, to Sister Agnes Louise for teaching me how to do God's Work. And finally, to Sister Theresa Maria and the others labouring long hours helping abandoned, unmarried pregnant females. These ladies loved the Holy Family and worked tirelessly in spreading unconditional love to those in need.

They departed their mortal shells long ago, but they live in my heart still. Some days I feel them around me, especially Anna Marie, and tears flow down my cheeks. I love her more than anyone can imagine, an eternal love.

I am sure the sisters are training little angels to become good humans, helping the

Holy Family bring all those who want to return home to do so.

I try to do the same. I think Anna Marie is pleased with *su dulce amor* for fulfilling his death bed promise to her and God.

This tale is part of a Miracle the Holy Family has for humanity. An ancient love story passed from Christ to Miriam of Magdala and the Beloved Disciple to preserve, guard, and pass down, eventually to me. It is up to us to bring the Miracle to Fruition. How? Simply by sharing this tale with those God brings your way and learning to love each other. God speed, everyone.

Table of Contents

Note From the Author

Though this book is satisfactory for middle schoolers and above, the Epilogue may be complicated for younger readers to understand. In that case, I suggest skipping it and reading only the first three chapters. Very young ones, unable to read and with short attention spans, may enjoy hearing an abridged tale suited to their ages. Being still close to God, they will understand in their hearts.

One added benefit of this tome is that the three chapters are easily adapted into a three-week series of church sermons stressing Christ's Teachings on unconditional love.

Another potential use for this book is to present the story in Sunday school over three weeks. It shouldn't be challenging to come up with some age-appropriate questions and corresponding scripture readings.

I would love to find one or two experienced Sunday school teachers to work with me, creating a Sunday school workbook for publication and distribution.

Chapter 1

Nouseum: The City of God

Once upon a time, thousands of universes ago, God's Greatest Miracle occurred. Here is how it happened.

A Storyteller travelled through an unknown country for forty days and nights, prior to arriving outside a magnificent city. It was so splendid and stunning that the Storyteller stopped in awe. The city walls had been built using gold and silver bricks studded with every jewel one can imagine. Everywhere, cut diamonds sparkled in brilliant hues as the sunlight refracted off their facets. Flower and fruit trees providing shade and delicious treats. Exquisite fragrances of rose, gardenia, and osmanthus perfuming the city's air.

The Storyteller had never seen nor heard of such an august city.

Entering through the central city entrance, he notices no gates to close to keep enemies out. Many people greet the Storyteller, shaking his hand, and offering fruit, tea, coffee, cake, pastry, and other lovely things. Everyone is singing, laughing, and working happily.

Nowhere does he see poverty, sickness, meanness, or greed. All the people wear silk finery and jewels. But no one seems vain or greedy.

It surprises him as none of the doors to the houses have locks. He continues his tour of the city, eventually arriving at the city centre. In front of him stands a jolly old man with a white beard reaching almost to the ground.

The old man says to the Storyteller, "Greetings, Friend. I see your heart brought you to our fair City, even to the portals of the House of our beloved Prince and Princess."

The Storyteller doesn't know what to say.

Chuckling, the old man says, "I see you don't know why you are here?"

The Storyteller's tongue still cannot find any words.

"No one visits our city unless they have received an invitation from our beloved Prince and Princess."

The Storyteller stands there, confused.

Before he knew what happened, he finds himself inside a beautiful garden full of blooming bushes and gurgling fountains. Standing in front of him is a young couple dressed in simple clothes, without jewels or ornamentations

The old man introduces the Storyteller to the Prince and the Princess. They all sit down.

The Prince radiates divine presence and compassion. His hair is long, curly, and blond. His eyes are deep blue.

For a short moment, the Storyteller imagines that he is looking at an Angel Icon from the Eastern Church in Constantinople. Immediately he makes the Sign of the Cross and bows his head.

Looking up the Storyteller's eyes meet those of the Prince. The Storyteller feels the Prince's gaze opening a hidden tunnel leading deep into his own secret heart.

The Storyteller peers into the centre of his being, seeing himself as he truly is for the first time. He sees his mind as an enormous battlefield wherein wages an epic battle between egoism and altruism, evil and good. Two forces, angelic altruism and demonic selfishness, are at war with each other.

One warrior is a beautiful angel with flowing brown hair. The other is a hideous, selfish, demonic human ego created by biological evolution and socialisation.

The Storyteller feels overwhelmed, his mind full of conflicting feelings and thoughts. How often the ugly overpowers the beautiful because he allows it.

Suddenly, the Storyteller experiences the grievous suffering and unfairness of the human world. Copious tears fall from his eyes as he laments with every man, woman, and child. His sorrow rapidly increasing until it becomes unbearable. Finally, the Storyteller realises the great gulf separating who he could be and who he had been.

At his moment of most profound grief, the beautiful Princess, with her long raven-black hair and green eyes, looks deeply into his eyes. All the sorrow and pain vanishing, replaced with new feelings of peace, security, and joy as he experiences the Kingdom of Heaven Within. He realises Nouseum is the Eternal City of God. Now you know where

St. Augustine found inspiration for his 4th Century classic, The City of God.

The Storyteller realises that forgiveness is possible, even for those failing to live life skilfully or wholesomely. One must face the Archangel Michael, the Guardian of the Threshold, with courage and honesty.

He kneels on the grass and spreads out his arm to invite the Guardian into his heart.

He prays, "Come into me, Michael, Guardian and Messenger of True Conscience. Show me how to be born a second time. How to become a helper in the Work of the Creator-Absolute."

Michael appears before the Storyteller in a flash of blinding light.

Lowering his fearsome sword, Michael asks, "Do you wish in your Heart of Hearts to change from selfishness to altruism?

"Will you make an essence promise in the Name of the Holy Ones to listen to the angel within?

"To assume the mantel of a helper of God?

"If you sincerely see your past life errors and are strong enough to swear an essence promise, the forgiveness of Grace is yours. And with Grace comes Metanoia. God speed, Brother."

The Storyteller's vision clears, and he sees a soft violet light surrounding the Prince and Princess.

He asks, "Is it true? Am I truly forgiven? Am I now a helper of God?"

The Prince answers, "Yes, Storyteller. Your psychic heart is now living within our One heart."

The Princess says, "Friend, we had good reason to invite you to our beautiful City. But first, I think we should tell you a bit about who we are and where we are.

"In the past, others hearing about our city called it by many names. For example, in your world, people call it Shangri-La, Shambala, Avalon, Quivira, and Cíbola. Unfortunately, all these names and stories about our city are not accurate.

The proper name of our Grand City is Nouseum, after our city's inherent Nature. The people you have met are known as Those Whose Love and Wisdom are Always.

"You can think of our city as the Holy Conduit between the Love of the Creator-Absolute and the Kingdom of Heaven Within. Nouseum is the Holy City of God, for God established it long ago. It is not in Heaven but functions with the physical as an active arm of the Godhead. We exist to teach and inspire sentient beings on all planets to fulfil God's Plan. Our City is Eternal."

The Princess says, "Storyteller, we invited you into our home to share an incredible teaching tale—in the form of an eternal fairy tale. A love story you must learn and tell to all the children of your world.

"And one day, you must teach it to another storyteller. It is a tale meant for children-in-age and those becoming children once again in their Hearts as taught by Lord Yeshua. I am sure you all remember what Jesus said to his disciples in Matthew about the Kingdom of Heaven and God Within."

"The disciples came unto Jesus, saying, who is the greatest in the Kingdom of Heaven? And Jesus called a little child unto him and set him amidst them. Verily, I say unto you, except ye see conversion, and become as little children, ye shall not enter the Kingdom of Heaven. Whosoever humbles himself as this little child becomes the greatest in the Kingdom of Heaven. And whoso receives one such little child in my name, receives me. But whoso shall offend one of these little ones who trust implicitly in me; would be better off with a millstone hung about his neck and drowning in the sea's depth."

"We ask this favour of you, as we have asked innumerable storytellers dwelling in other places and other times. Only you can decide if you will help us help humanity."

The Prince says, "Friend, the story we are asking you to retell is how the Princess and I came to Nouseum. It is the story of why we come into every universe created by the Creator-Absolute. For our story is the story meant for men and women possessing noble hearts and rational minds. Our story is why Creator-Absolute manifested the Holy City of God. What say you?"

The Storyteller still finds no words. But as he sits within this serene garden in silence, he hears Lord Yeshua whispering the brilliant story into his inner ears. The story's events are as musical notes, each melodiously linked to those proceeding and following.

As he listens, he feels he is within the single Heart of the Prince and Princess. He understands this story contains the first and the last Chapters in the spiritual completion of humankind. This story is the Creator's never-ending Saga of Eternal Hope through Unconditional Love.

The Prince reaches out and places his right hand upon the shoulder of the Storyteller.

Grinning a broad and compassionate smile, the Prince says, "If your heart had not agreed to our request, our teaching tale would not be living there now. So go, dear Friend, tell the world about God's Greatest Miracle: A Tale of Two Little Angels. And someday, in the distant future, you will return to live in our fair city. As this time approaches, watch for other excellent storytellers and direct them to our city. Then, if they are ready, they will hear our call."

The Princess stood up and lightly kissed the Storyteller on the lips, saying, "Go, Child, tell the story so others may find the path to our fair land."

As her lips left his, the Storyteller finds himself no longer in the Great City of the Prince and Princess, but on the outskirts of a city, he knows. He enters through the gates, goes into the marketplace, and begins telling his wondrous tale. Soon children surround him; their Ears and Hearts open to their angels within.

A wise man standing nearby turns to his wife, saying, "My love, do you see the warm glow radiating from the Storyteller? He is a chosen One. The little ones understand automatically. Just like Our Lord taught so long ago."

"Yes, I see the glow. Our Lord is blessing us, Husband."

So, boys and girls, this is how our story begins.

Chapter 2

Heaven

Once upon an age, even before our earth existed, in another Universe, far away in space and time, we find ourselves in Heaven. We are at the Institute for the Creation of New Essence Personalities.

The angels working in this Institute are eternally experimenting with new recipes, formulas, and methodologies to bring new angels into existence. Even in Heaven, the angels use scientific method and the Higher Laws God placed within Nature.

It takes special skills to run the Institute for the Creation of New Essence Personalities. First, you must be a brilliant angel. One with an incredible imagination, thinking outside the typical day-to-day angel box, and not afraid to be wrong. Someone who has been around God since the beginning, a very experienced angel. An angel, such as the Archangel Raphael.

In the early days of the Institute, Raphael discovered that the best way for creating new Essence Personalities is as a pair of one boy and one girl angel. Such a discovery should not be surprising? Don't we observe that most animals come in two kinds, male and female, including those without Essence personalities?

One fine day, the Institute's geneticist engineers removed a particular set of boy-girl angels from the Essence Personality Energy Machine. Raphael was standing nearby, discussing an idea he had with his friend, the Archangel Michael.

Abruptly, both turned to look at the most recent pair of angel babies. The two Archangels noticed something unusual, something neither had seen before. Never in any other angel pair created for this universe or any previous one.

Typically, when you look at the new angel baby pair, you see two separate angel babies. But something strange was happening here. When you looked directly at each angel baby, you saw two distinct Essence personalities. But if you relaxed the focus of your eyes, the two angel babies blended into one, just for a split second, or even less.

Michael said to Raphael, "I think you and I had better watch after these two ourselves. Something significant has occurred, and we need to be on guard for further developments."

And so, dear boys and girls, this is exactly what Michael and Raphael did.

I should mention that even though angel babies come into existence as pairs, the pair members are no more related to each other than non-pair members. They grow up in separate angel families and attend different Human Training Schools. The goal is to prevent the boy-angel and girl-angel from meeting before human birthing. No one knows why? Except for God.

Little angel babies stay at home with their angel parents until they are two angel years old. At this age, they begin the first level of angel school. After that, they study until they are thirty-three angel months old when they come to earth to be reborn.

The little boy-angel was outspoken. Forever asking the more significant angels questions. Questions about things they rarely knew or cared to know.

"Why do we become humans? Why are angel babies made in pairs? How do physical universes come to be? What is the Essence Personality made of? How come we can't see God," and many, many more?

After a while, the more prominent angels avoided the little boy-angel.

They said to each other, "This little boy-angel is just too smart for his own good and will never amount to much, asking all these foolish questions. He just needs to get on with the program."

Maybe you are like the little boy-angel yourself? What do you think?

But don't worry. Asking questions about the universe and people around you is okay. But never, let the sleeping adults make you feel bad about being curious or asking questions. God and the Archangels approve of such behaviour if you are thinking of others. And don't forget, this applies to little girl-angels too.

The only angels taking the time to encourage our little boy-angel's searching and inquisitive nature were the Archangels Michael and Raphael. Whenever they were free from watching over their Institutes, and the little boy-angel was not in school, they would do pleasant things together. Yes, dear boys and girls, there is a school in Heaven!

Raphael would take the little boy-angel for nature hikes into the forests and fields surrounding the angel cities. As the two hiked, they would stop and observe the wonders of Nature in Heaven.

For example, the little boy-angel learned how the spirit-bees work together to make nourishing honey for the hive. How a spirit-crow grabs a hard nut in her beak and flies high into the sky and drops it onto a hard rock so it would crack, allowing the bird to extract the nutmeat.

Raphael and the little boy-angel sometimes sailed on the high seas, watching the antics of spirit-birds and spirit-flying fish. Sometimes they watched through a glass-bottomed jar to see spirit-crabs and spirit-starfish walking along the ocean's bottom. Other days, they would swim and play with the dolphins.

Often, Raphael and the boy-angel would visit Puff the Magic Dragon. They would don their sailing clothes and sail the magical seas rescuing young maidens from the pirates.

The boy-angel promised Puff that he would always be his best friend and they could live together one day in a Great City by the Great Sea. And Nouseum is by the Great Sea.

Raphael and the little boy-angel looked forward to these fascinating journeys, even if the other big angels thought it somewhat foolish.

Some days, Raphael would bring the little boy-angel to his Institute and explain how angel babies come in being. Occasionally, the little boy-angel could push the buttons on the Essence Personality Energy Machine. He always listened to Raphael's instructions, well, at least at the Institute. They were good friends.

* * *

Michael differs from Raphael. He is the chief military general in Heaven, the right arm of the Creator-Absolute. He is the Guardian of the Way Lord Yeshua gave to sentient creatures to transform themselves into *Homo dei*. But there has been no mischief for an eternity of time. Now he helps sentient creatures in the physical worlds become fully conscious. Michael teaches people to be awake, understanding, reliable, fearless, and fair, even with selfish and arrogant people.

Unfortunately, some people aren't amicable and do nasty things. They behave this way because they are greedy, hateful, and perplexed. This unfortunate event occurs because such persons allow the animal side of their nature to be in charge rather than the angel. The animal side wants everything for its benefit. The animal side is crafty. It is the thinking and feeling machine God gives to us to distinguish between selfishness and kindness.

However, Creator-Absolute does not want us to remain like animals. Learning to be kind and responsible for our actions is what God desires for us. God wants us to become as God is Itself by using our Divine gift to choose between conflicting alternatives. Hopefully, deciding to act wholesomely and skilfully while in a physical body.

Your parents and teachers should help you learn to be thoughtful towards the earth and all living things. After all, Adam and Eve were the first stewards of the Garden of Eden.

We no longer live in the Garden of Eden. Still, we are responsible for caring for the earthly garden Creator-Absolute provides us. We must become stewards of our beautiful planet, loving and preserving it from harm to its air, water, soil, plants, and animals. Genuine caring for all life is natural to the angel within; it is not so with our ever-consuming biological creature.

Selfish people never learn how to listen to the angel within. Sometimes people become so uncaring and nasty that the angel within loses its resonance bond with the vehicle and returns to Heaven, leaving the person no better off than a clever and dangerous animal. It happens more than you might think?

The failure of an Essence Personality to remain on earth is sad. But God will never allow the vehicle to corrupt the angel within. It is a Divine Law. A few storytellers tell stories of angels rebelling against Creator-Absolute in Heaven, but these stories aren't necessary now. The only rebellion is the vehicle against the angel within.

A bit of rebellion helps our human ego learn about God's Plan for the universe and our role in the Divine Play. Without some conflict between the angel and the animal, the animal would never accept its angel's Authority within, nor would the angel within be growing in wisdom and beingness.

So, allow me to tell you what happens in a new Universe.

First come photons and plasma, atoms, molecules, cells, multicellular organisms, worms, fish, etc. Then monkeys, then primates, then primitive humans, and finally, modern man. Thus, the evolving complexity of being and mind guided by God's immutable Laws; and God's Plan established in the universe before ours.

Essence Personalities can only communicate and guide their human egos when the physical body is born with a properly functioning brain, intellectually and ethically. The human mind needs to recognise the angel's presence and intentionally allow it to be its guide.

If the human brain is defective, as happens with sociopaths, there is no angel within. The person exists only in the savage world of the worst kind of egoism. These people cause much unnecessary harm to those who live life as good householders.

You see boys and girls, how important it is to pay attention to your angel within, even if your angel is still young.

The Archangel Gabriel will explain what I just said during a Human Training School class a little later. Each of you needs to pay attention and listen so the angel within may remember, and the ego may learn.

Once Michael was out of his office, the Institute for the Final Development of a Conscious Essence Personality, the little boy-angel snuck in and tried to handle Michael's Great War sword. Of course, we all know one should not play with other people's property without asking permission. Doing so is impolite and inconsiderate. But little boy-angels are much like little human boys, sometimes up to mischief.

Michael's sword is so heavy that he is the only angel in Heaven who can wield it, lift, and use it. Maybe someone could pull it out of its scabbard but raise it; no way, it is too heavy.

The boy-angel had to place a chair beneath it to reach the sword.

Just as the little boy-angel pulled on the Sword, Michael strolled into the office and saw the little boy-angel.

"That is my Sword. Didn't I tell you never to touch it?"

Startled by Michael, the little boy-angel jumped and pulled the sword from its sheath. The little boy-angel held the blade as if it weighed no more than a fork or spoon! Michael couldn't believe his very own eyes.

Silently and gazing somewhat downwards towards the floor, the boy-angel handed the sword to Michael. Michael took it and replaced it into the scabbard on the wall next to his chain mail armour and shield.

The little boy-angel replied, "I am sorry. I just wanted to be like you."

Trying his best not to smile, Michael grabbed the little boy-angel by the collar of his coat and placed him on the floor.

"You could have cut yourself with my sword, Tristan. So don't touch it ever again, okay?"

The little boy-angel nodded his head and gave Michael a big hug, saying, "I am sorry. I love you."

And with that, he ran out the door as Michael broke into a loud, hearty laugh, "That child, I can hardly wait until he is born into the earthly realms."

* * *

Now, the little girl-angel was the opposite of the little boy-angel. Although the little girl-angel asked many questions, she did so pleasantly, and she always helped the big angels.

The older angels often noted just how different these two angel children were. A bizarre situation, considering they came from the same angel mould. One would think they would have more behaviours in common?

Raphael and Michael spent as much time with the little girl-angel as they did with the little boy. However, they never spent time together with both. God had established this rule a long time ago. No one knew why?

The lady Archangel Ariel was fond of the little-girl angel. She taught her many valuable things about the physical universe. She explained all about flowers, plants, and animals, how people grow food, how doctors and nurses work to keep people healthy, and much more.

Ariel hoped that the little girl-angel would be of great use to the world after becoming human.

* * *

One day, summer was over, and it was time to begin the final Human Training School class. Since I brought up the Human

Training School subject, we need to listen to one of the introductory lectures given to angel children in their first school course. Don't be surprised if it feels like you have heard this before, for most of you have an angel within who might remember?

So, imagine you are back in angel school sitting at your desk with all your friends. Your professor, Gabriel, enters the room. He is tall, handsome, and sure of himself. But everyone is quiet, for all of you realise Gabriel is the Messenger for God. One of his jobs is to tell people on earth what the Creator-Absolute desires of them. There are stories in the Bible and Koran about Gabriel.

As was often the case, the little boy-angel was running somewhat late, for he had stopped to watch some spirit frogs hopping around their stream.

Realising he was late, he ran to school, entering the wrong classroom door. He saw the little girl-angel for the first time since their creation as he came through the door. The little girl-angel's presence mesmerised the little boy-angel. Morgana was so sweet and pretty with her long, straight black hair and emerald-green eyes. She wore a bright white starched school dress.

He tripped, striking his forehead on the teacher's desk corner, as he was not paying attention to where he walked. He gashed his forehead just above his left eye and started to cry.

The little girl-angel jumped out of her chair and ran to the little boy-angel and placed her handkerchief over his wound, saying, "Don't cry. I'll take care of you."

As she applied pressure to the cut to stop the bleeding, she placed his head into her lap. At that moment, their eyes found each other, green merging with blue. They knew they were a pair and would fast be friends.

Gabriel rose from his desk and asked, "Are you okay, Tristan? Morgana surely knows her first aid. Morgana, show our little friend to a seat, please. Since he is here, Tristan might as well remain in our class."

Our story is becoming even more curious. I wonder why Gabriel allowed Tristan to stay in the same class as Morgana? Does Gabriel know something we don't know? Is this part of Creator-Absolute's experiments? What do you think, boys and girls?

Morgana helped the boy to his seat, which was next to her desk.

After everyone settled down, Gabriel began, "Boys and girls, I hope you have been practising being considerate. You must establish this habit while in Heaven. You will find it is difficult to get your human body and brain to do what God would like as their design is to obey physical demands."

One girl-angel raised her hand, asking, "Gabriel, why will it be hard to get our human body and brain to do what God wants us to do?"

"Good question, Constance. First, the human creature will be a baby who needs to function in an unfamiliar environment. The baby must learn to sit, walk, and talk. The baby will take many years to grow to learn how to behave appropriately. During this early life period, you will sleep until the baby reaches a responsible age.

"Still, you are essential, for you are what we call Essence—that something responsible for counteracting the human biological drives to preserve self, physical and mental, and hoarding. The Essence moves from life to life in those who are reborn as God's helpers. The human body and mind are temporary but necessary vehicles for angels to evolve in awareness and beingness to come closer to the Creator-Absolute.

"Our System uses the term Essence to represent the angel within, for such an actuality is necessary, or essential, for accomplishing a valuable endpoint for our physical universe. The Buddhist Yogacara school calls it container-consciousness. Christian-Islamic schools call it the soul. Indian schools use terms such as Jiva, Atma, and Bhagavat.

"So, remember, a name is less important than understanding a concept or a reality. Avoid arguing over names as it leads us away from love and caring.

"Our friend Lord Yeshua gets gravely upset when people argue and fight over his Teachings. Such violence and concupiscence in his name break his dear heart. He is disappointed that his Pristine Church became a haven for greedy and power-seeking individuals worshipping one or more demonic archetypes.

"After the age of thirteen years, Essence may awaken to its residence in the body, allowing it to interact with the mind and emotions of the body. As a result, Essence realises what the human is thinking, feeling, and doing. While the mind-brain does not know it, Essence forms a portion of the human consciousness. Thus, Essence manifests as the beginning of the true I.

"As the angel within gains increased experience in life, he or she awakens at younger ages, sometimes as early as eighteen months for a Holy Master or Mistress.

"Even though the body calls itself, I, whenever it authors an action, it is only a Me, a psychobiological creature of evolution. The sense of Me-ness is vital for physical and mental survival. One needs to understand who begins an action and who receives the consequences. A person needs to possess a feeling of psychological existence, a Me. This way, as an agent, it can experience its conditioned choices' mental and physical effects. No human zombies are allowed.

"Every sentient creature, like human beings, must suffer discomfort, intolerance, fear, anxiety, joy, and other conscious emotions. If Creator-Absolute created perfect sentient creatures, they could not understand why altruism is preferable to egoism—for all their actions would be automatic. Nevertheless, it can learn how to put aside selfish desires and replace them with generosity.

"Failing to possess the ability to choose how to respond to a situation or realise our evolution's endpoint and purpose, we would be biological machines, *Homo insectus*. Thus, never understanding ***why perfected human love is what God wants for us the most.***

"If our universe was a perfect creation, nothing new and better could evolve, for it would end in the same condition as it started. Therefore, such a world is static and unchanging.

"Creator-Absolute desires sentient creatures to arise from biological evolution and become unique spiritual beings. Beings united in Intentions and Will, individual and united in Essence and Action, one of Many and many of One, easy to experience though difficult to describe."

A boy-angel asks, "Gabriel, I understand what you are teaching, but do we change and grow from interacting with a human body and suffering what it suffers?"

"Arthur, another good question. Suppose you establish an excellent rapport with your body so that the ego listens to your urgings. In that case, you and the ego will resonate and work together to rid the ego of unnecessary and unwholesome personas and drives. The closer the ego resonates with the angel within, the more the angel grows in conscious awareness and beingness.

"It is difficult to explain. When you are in Heaven, your true I is fully functional. It operates on the level of knowledge and beingness gained through sequential physical lives. Therefore, angels of different ages live in Heaven—babies, infants, toddlers, and so on up to thirty-three years of age.

"After reincarnating in the material world many times, your Essence will manifest earlier in the creature's life. For the ego and Essence are in harmonious resonance and more accessible to each other. You need to realise that the creature functions from two competing points of view and will—either the true I or the mortal ego. The result is that the human machine acts as commanded by the true I or by the human ego's controlling desires.

"Your long-term goal is to marry the mortal I and the true I so that only one individual exists. The Masters denote this state of existence by the term enlightenment. Enlightened angel-egos are said to live within the Kingdom of Heaven in the West or in

Nirvana with residue in the East. Same state, different names.

"Expect little progress in your first incarnation, as you will lack experience in communicating with the human ego. However, you will improve as you learn from living life in the physical realms.

"The Creator-Absolute desires each of you to awaken by understanding the critical differences between egoism and altruism and act accordingly.

"This eventual goal of reincarnating is the healthy development of your angel-ego by gradually guiding the mortal-ego away from its evolutionary state of egoism and greed (the dark) into its dormant state of enlightenment and altruism (the light). Thus, your angelic characteristics lie dormant within your Essence until activated and expressed by one of the resident personas comprising your physical vehicle's mind.

"People think they have one personality when all of us exist with many personas. These personas take turns occupying the brain control centre—these personas, or ego-states, created after birth into the physical world to live within the personality family. Most people are not objectively aware of how many personas they unconsciously adopted as they grew up and now exist within.

"If you pay close attention to your vehicle, you discover it is born with specific characteristics and aspects associated with its personality family. These characteristics are both innate and enduring. For example, anxious infants are the same way when they are older.

What we call temperament is our vehicle's psychobiological potential to express specific emotional traits and personality types. Temperament is challenging to change, so you must learn to direct it toward healthy rather than selfish ends.

"So, the angel ego's job is to locate and support one of the advanced personas within the personality family. This ego-state resonates with your angel ego. We call this persona Deputy Steward.

"Most humans possess a Deputy Steward naturally, for Deputy Steward resonates with the angel within as established by God at the beginning of animal evolution. Careful observation of advanced animals shows us various altruistic behaviours in wolves, dogs, dolphins, apes, and other advanced animals.

"I hope you can see the wisdom of creation; how Creator-Absolute provided the higher animals with a 'touch of angelic energies' to prepare a Deputy Steward foundation in sentient creatures.

Some people think our human personas travel from life to life during reincarnation. This theory is incorrect. Each physical incarnation comes with its own set of personas and drives derived from our social environments.

The only persona capable of moving between lives is Deputy Steward. Deputy Steward is the aphysical transport container or vehicle utilized by authentic I. It is our link between the spiritual character of the human mind and the angel within.

The Eastern Schools call the Deputy Steward the container for consciousness.

"Once Deputy Steward occupies the neurological control centre, it can enlist the help of resonating personas to re-educate or remove those personas who are unwilling to serve the higher good.

"Eventually, Deputy Steward refines and unifies the personality family, allowing the angel within to take its throne in the control centre and rule the vehicle wisely. Hence, the angel we call Steward.

"Therefore, we can say that the enlightened angel within is both human and angel and will remain so from then on, serving as a Master and Avatar to Humanity. Once an angel is a Master, the body it inhabits is the crème de la crème, naturally attuned to the Master's qualities and work. Such vehicles awaken to the angel within soon after the first year of physical life.

"Our friend Lord Yeshua is an example of such a Master. His final earthly form was as the Prophet Enoch. The Creator-Absolute brought his person to Heaven and adopted Enoch as his Son Metatron. Metatron volunteered to return to earth as the Christ to redeem humanity and fulfil God's Plan. Enoch is one of two enlightened human beings elevated to Archangels.

"I think this is sufficient for the morning's class. Please, Morgana, bring Tristan up to my desk so I can heal his cut."

And dear Morgana and Tristan went to Gabriel's desk.

Chapter 3

Perfected Human Love

From that first day in class onward, the little boy-angel and the little girl-angel were inseparable. They were always doing something together. For example, the little boy-angel brought her on his hikes with Raphael. The little girl-angel taught him about first aid and how to ask questions nicely. Often, they held each other's hands.

Sometimes when they were together, the other angels noticed it became difficult to tell them apart. Not that they looked similar, for they didn't. Still, their energies seemed to blend as if only one angelic power was present, like purple, after mixing blue and red pigments. Everyone thought it mysterious.

Eventually, it came time for the angel children to graduate and prepare for birth as baby human bodies. But unfortunately, while the other angel children were ecstatic about the opportunity, the little girl-angel and little boy-angel weren't happy at all.

They loved each other, were terrific friends, did not want to part company, and did not want to be born human babies. They had learned in class that graduates of the same course never meet each other until they return to Heaven as earthly angels. Well, boys and girls, this is the standard rule, as we learned.

So, the little girl-angel said to the little boy-angel, "Tristan, you and I must run away and hide in the forest with the elves. They are our friends and will not tell where we are. I don't want to lose you, for I love you so dearly. Do you agree?"

The little boy-angel replies, "You are so smart, Morgana. Let us leave now."

The two of them ran far away to the land of the elves to hide. As this land was closer to the isle of perpetual ice, the little angels brought warm clothing. Every night, the boy-angel would build a soft bed of leaves for the two of them. He made sure that he kept the little girl-angel warm by giving her the extra blanket and holding her in his arms. They ate tubers and fruits from the forest.

When Michael and Raphael found out they were missing, they knew they had run off to the elves. It took about a week to find the little angels.

Neither Michael nor Raphael were angry with the runaways. Instead, they told the little girl-angel and the little boy-angel that they would help them as best they could. They calmly explained that they had to be born because God established this good rule long ago. It seemed to work well.

Therefore, Michael went to speak with the Archangel in charge of the Institute for the Human Birthing of Angel Children. We met her before, and her name is Ariel. Usually, the angels working with Ariel had full responsibility for finding the proper human bodies for each of the angel children. This procedure had always been so.

Therefore, when Michael suggested it would be a good idea for Ariel to allow him to place these two angel children in human bodies, she baulked at the thought.

"Humbug," she said, "I never heard of a more absurd idea in all the aeons I have been doing this job. No way, Michael."

Now, Michael is handsome and can be most charming and persuasive when he wants to be. He whispered something into Ariel's ear; she laughed and agreed to his suggestion. He would take personal charge of this birthing experience.

Dear boys and girls, what do you think Michael whispered to Ariel?

So, the time came for our dear friends, the little girl-angel and little-boy angel, to be born into the earthly realms, and Michael did as he promised, much to the delight of Ariel. Soon you will see why Ariel was so happy.

* * *

The little boy-angel was born into the family of a kind King and Queen. They lived in a small province far out in the country. It was a charming place as it had lakes, forests, fields, animals, and plants. The residents of this land were kind and industrious. The Little Prince liked where he lived.

When he was about three years old, a wealthy merchant family travelled from far across the seas to live in the Kingdom, and the little boy walked over to meet them. As he neared the estate walls, he heard a little girl's voice emanating from within.

The Little Prince thought it adorable and climbed the apple tree growing next to the wall. He climbed up the tree, crawling out onto a branch so he could see the little girl.

She wore a white dress and black shoes. She spoke to a black-grey dodo bird wearing spectacles, an orange top hat, and a white rabbit in a red vest with a golden braid.

The Little Prince couldn't believe his eyes and crawled out further on the limb. Boom. The branch cracked, and the little boy fell into the yard, hitting his head on a rock and causing a gash over his left eye.

The Little Prince began to cry, and the little girl took out a handkerchief and ran over to him, taking his head into her lap; she did her best to stop the bleeding.

"Don't cry, little boy. It will be all right. I'll take care of you."

And that was that. From that moment onward, these two were always together, the best of friends, even though they had forgotten that they had known each other as angel children, as God said must be.

It may seem strange that the little boy-angel and little girl-angel met each other as human beings. But wasn't there a rule about never meeting on earth? Hum?

The Little Prince often brought the little girl colourful flowers and pretty stones. They went on long hikes into the woods, never getting lost, for the little boy had an uncanny sense of direction. They listened to the birds speaking to each other, and the little girl would tell the little boy what they said. Sometimes they played games with unicorns and elves, accompanying them on magical journeys. The little girl showed the little boy how to cook over a campfire and mend hurt animals.

Sometimes their parents visited each other. Invariably, they commented on how sweet they were to each other—never arguing and always making space for the other's needs and moods. What a perfect pair they are.

The parents often remarked to each other, "Surely, this relationship must have begun in Heaven."

One day after school, when the two children were six years old, the Little Prince came to the little girl's house and softly knocked. He wasn't as loud and abrupt as in the past, for he learned how to be more considerate from the little girl.

The little girl's mother opened the door.

"Little Prince," she said, "our daughter is sick and cannot see you today. Come back tomorrow."

The little boy came back every day for a month. Each day the little girl's mother said, "Not today, Little Prince, maybe tomorrow."

The mother looked sad and haggard to the little boy, and he was much concerned about the little girl.

The Little Prince asked his parents, "Mummy, why is Morgana sick? I am worried, and it makes me cry at night."

His parents could not tell him why, but they worried too.

Then one day, after knocking upon the door, the little girl's mother said, "You can come in today, Little Prince, and visit with Morgana. She seems stronger."

Tristan ran excitedly into the little girl's room. She was so thin, and her complexion as pale as milk.

But he smiled the biggest smile he could make, giving the little girl a big hug and a kiss on her lips.

"I've missed you so very much. I love you little girl. Are you okay?"

For the first time in many days, the little girl smiled, hugging the little boy back.

"Now that you are here, I am fine; I love you, Little Prince."

Every day, the little boy visited the little girl after school. He read stories, wrote funny poems, and brought her fruits and nuts, even though her appetite was feeble. Everything he could do, he did for the little girl.

He loved the little girl with all his heart and wished she would get better soon to play with the elves and unicorns. But she grew weaker and paler as the days came and went.

Once the little boy visited, and the little girl told him that an angel with a flaming sword had seen her last night.

The angel said, "Morgana, I knew you and Tristan when both of you were still angel children. When I brought you to earth to be born, I choose the human bodies you both were to have. It worried me you two would never meet, but you did! Miracles of Miracles. Wonders of Wonders.

"Since I had a premonition that you might get sick one day when still a child, I found another little girl who looks exactly like you and placed part of your Essence into her, just in case.

"You two are part of a grand experiment, a brand-new experiment. So, when you take your last breath, your portion of your Essence will pass onto this other little girl, and both will be as one. Tell the little boy that he must never stop looking until he finds you. No matter how many years it might take."

This day was the last time the Little Prince saw his true love, for Essence left her body that night and passed into the other little girl. The Little Prince cried and cried, even after he grew up into a handsome Prince. Whenever the Prince was not busy, memories of the little girl entered his awareness. He missed her so much.

* * *

When the little boy grew up, he left his lands to his younger brother and sister, becoming a physician and alchemist. He travelled all over his planet, helping the disadvantaged and oppressed. But, he wasn't popular with many of the kings and dictators of the world. Nor with many of the wealthy persons.

The farmers, the shepherds, the holy men, the sailors, the grannies, the children, and all the poor and hard-working people loved the Prince dearly. He became known as a powerful advocate for ensuring good. He was ready to stand up for any oppressed person at a moment's notice. Because he loved the people, they knew that he genuinely was a Prince given to them by God.

But when he was alone at night or travelling to a new land, he remembered the little girl and cried softly to himself, for he missed her more than anything else. He felt consoled in his heart, knowing that she would be happy knowing of his work.

Now a grown-up Prince, the Little Prince searched for the other little girl, now an adult.

One day, the Prince visited a great city in a foreign country built by a harbour leading to the Great Sea. He sat at a table with several old scriptural books resting on its top. As he waited for his meal, he enjoyed smelling the sea air and watching the frigatebirds fish.

He thought to himself, "If only people could soar like the frigatebirds and know the true freedom that God gave to all of us."

As he turned his head, he saw the most beautiful woman he had ever seen walking into the restaurant. He recognised her immediately; it was the little girl all grown up. Even though the Prince knew her, she did not recognise him.

He arose from his table and graciously introduced himself to the lady, careful not to say too much.

"My name is Tristan, dear lady. What is your name? If I may ask?"

"My name is Morgana. Please join me for dinner?"

Tristan sat down, and they talked about their lives for several hours as glorious Moon Maiden rose in the sky.

The woman felt as if she had known the man all her life, though she knew they had never met. Her heart told her he was a Prince sent by God. They had much in common, as she was also a physician travelling the world, helping the poor, the meek, and the set upon.

Following this meeting, the man and the woman spent many months getting to know each other. They travelled the world together, caring for the sick, assuring that everyone had healthy food to eat, and clean water to drink. They created schools to educate the poor children so someday they could help themselves, their families, and free their countries of dictators and other nasty persons.

The grown-up little boy and the little girl became famous worldwide, but they never became proud, arrogant, or greedy. They just enjoyed being kind to others. Doing what God wanted together was sufficient for them.

They sound a little like Robin Hood and Maid Marian, don't they?

If the land ruler was jealous, greedy, or hateful, he would send soldiers to capture the pair. But, no matter how crafty the ruler was, the Prince was cleverer. No one would hurt his beloved, nor keep them from helping all the friends they met on their travels.

They would often go into remote areas ravaged by deadly and contagious diseases to tend to the local people. Places no one else dared visit for fear of dying.

Once, someone asked the grown-up little angel girl, "Aren't you afraid of catching one of these diseases and dying?"

"Oh, we never worry about that, for we always have too much work to do. Sometimes it almost feels as the angels are keeping us safe."

One night, when the moon was full and shining brightly on the planet, the Prince turned and looked with tearful eyes at his beloved, and she remembered the little boy. She remembered all the time they had spent together and how much they loved each other. How her other half had died and how her portion of Essence passed into her.

Tears welled in her eyes as she hugged and kissed her Prince.

"I understand everything now, my love. I know who I am and how we came to be together. It feels like the south wind blew away a dark cloud, keeping me from seeing my past. Truly, ***I now understand the power present with the perfection of human love.*** I love you, all the way to God, and perhaps, even further if possible."

As she spoke, her eyes glowed with the light of Heaven.

"Love of my existence, now that you remember everything, I think it is time to marry."

It was the proper time for them to get married, and they did just that.

* * *

Soon they formed a unique school upon their earth called the Institute for Conscious Evolution and Human Development. Sounds like Michael's Institute, doesn't it?

And they accepted students into the new school. The first were university students who had not yet hushed the voice of the angel within. They quickly came to appreciate the message taught by the angelic Prince and Princess—the necessity of awakening your material personality to its associated Essence Personality to become a conscious helper of God on Earth.

Later came the first older adults, and some even brought their children. All of them, slowly learning what it means to live a life of Unconditional Love and Compassion—learning to Work and Help all peoples of the world for the sake of God and the world.

The school grew under their influence. Its students prospered under the loving guidance of the two earthly angels—many healing events manifesting in the world because of the school's activities. The school was the catalyst, the lens collecting, concentrating, and radiating God's Pure Love into the challenging world.

As a result, there was less war, less hunger, less hate, and fewer defective human machines causing harm and pain every year. But how this happened, I must leave for another story.

A long time on earth had passed for the little boy and the little girl. They both had reached the unheard-of age of 129 years. They had a charming home on the beach near a clear, blue lagoon in the South Islands. It was beautiful and very peaceful. A perfect place to retire to, for both needed a rest.

They moved here because all the people of the new earth asked them to become Emperor and Empress.

The Princess answered, "This is not right. You must learn to choose the wise ones to help guide you and move you into your futures."

The people finally agreed but told them, you will always be our beloved Prince and Princess.

And all were happy and content.

As they sat together on beach lounges looking out over the blue ocean, the surface was as calm as a mirror's face sparkling with the bright sky orange light of the setting sun.

Morgana turned her head and looked lovingly at her beloved Tristan.

She asked, "Tristan, dearest love of my life and Essence, are you sad because I could not give you children of our own to love and teach?"

Tristan reached out and took his beloved's hand in his own.

"Morgana, how could I be sad about anything being next to you all these many years? You know that all the world's peoples are our children, big and small, rich and poor, black and white and yellow. We have watched them grow so big, reaching high into the Heavens for God.

"Imagine all the students who learned to love each other, just as we love each other without limitations, selfishness, and compassion. No, darling, I am not sad. We just didn't have time, I guess. I love you, little girl, and always will."

Morgana smiled, squeezing the Prince's hand even tighter as joyful tears fall from her eyes. Not being able to have babies had bothered her for so many years.

She thought to herself, "I have the best husband and friend in all the world. My heart knows his love for me is pure and unconditional, as is my love for him."

"Wife, I think it is time for us to complete this journey and move onward. Take my hand and hold tight; it is time for us to rest and sleep until God has more work. Our students can continue the work we began with the Institute for Conscious Evolution and Human Development. Sometimes I think we trained them to be even more effective than ourselves. I'm glad we did. Rest, Heart of my Heart, rest well."

The pair of saints fell into a sound sleep, exhaling their last breaths in unison. Their Essence Personalities withdrew from the tired bodies and passed into Heaven.

* * *

When they awoke, they saw and recognised their old friends. Raphael and Michael. None had changed in appearance. When they looked at each other, they no longer had grey hair and wrinkles but saw themselves as when they met at the restaurant. They were no longer angel children.

Raphael said, "We are so proud of you two. Aren't we, Michael?"

Michael grinned and nodded in agreement, saying, "No one ever thought such a thing could happen. Imagine two humans learning to love each other unconditionally in a single life—both of you growing from young angel children into mature adults in only one incarnation.

"I know you came from a unique formula, but that was not enough. You did it by committing yourselves to live life as God meant us to live. As a result, you became fully conscious and present in the world. You took on impossible labour and made enlightenment an actuality for others. Verily, this is God's Greatest Miracle."

Ariel arrived, having just finished placing a new class of angel babies in human bodies.

She kissed them both on the lips, saying, "Michael, you were right in convincing me to allow you to intervene in their placement on earth. We learned something fundamental that we can use to produce stronger and more effective angel babies, bringing a little more peace and mercy to the other worlds."

From Nowhere and from Everywhere, a Grand Voice filled the Heavens of all the Universes, "You have done well, my children, very well. I've waited for such a long time for two incarnating Essence Personalities to discover how to love each other without limitations or restrictions. To show unconditional love to every person in the world below. ***A passion for unconditional Love, Love perfected through personal effort and sacrifice working in the physical world.***

"Finally, all is as it should be. You are both ready to come to stay with me at my home. You are the first to have completed the journey and earned the right to enter my direct Abode. What do you think?"

The two angels, who weren't so little anymore, looked deep into each other's eyes, communicating through two Hearts joined as one. Finally, they decided on one unified Intention.

Morgana said, "Lord, if you don't mind, we would rather stay here and watch out for and teach the little angels more about your Grand Plan and how to achieve it."

Tristan added, "Lord, you know how things fall apart whenever one stops putting effort into them. We want to make sure everything continues to function correctly. Plus, if we move to your home, who will be available to supervise the formation of new schools in other Universes? There is a great need for that, you know. We hope this is okay?"

Again, from out of Nowhere and Everywhere, the Voice declared, "I hoped you might decide this way, my dear Prince and Princess. For such, you are henceforth here and within every universe. For you are the first of what shall be Bodhisattvas. A most enlightening concept describing angels who return to earth to guide others in awakening their angels within.

"And yes, you are correct. The school you actualised will serve as the foundation hearth for a Great Brotherhood. A Brotherhood for radiating Light, Life, and Love to all sentient beings. A Brotherhood for establishing Sacred Schools in every future universe, teaching the Way of the Gallant Heart.

"I will give you a Great City where all your future Bodhisattvas and Storytellers may live. This City, I name Nouseum. It will manifest within every future universe. It will be a beacon of light guiding all sentient beings as they find their path out of the Forest of Errors. Nouseum is the City of God."

And with that, the angels heard a soft laugh of Sublime delight resounding throughout all the Universes. All the angels smiled, rejoicing in their Hearts, feeling closer to each other than they had ever felt before. Raphael even noticed that Ariel and Michael were holding hands.

* * *

Dear children, we have come to the end of the story, or maybe it is just the beginning. Learning how to love each other is by far the most challenging task in any Universe. But, if we all work a little harder, maybe we can be like the little boy and the little girl angels? Perhaps we can study and one day become Storytellers and Bodhisattvas? What do you think?

Goodbye, little friends. Try to love each other and never be afraid to stand up for things you feel in your heart are what God asks you to do. Are you going to do your very best? I think you know in your innermost heart; you are sincere and just. See you someday in the Great City, Nouseum.

Best Wishes and Much Love, your Storyteller and Eternal Friend,

Jean-Michel

Cc: Prince Tristan and Princess Morgana, the Great City Palace, Nouseum, The Elfin Forever Land

Epilogue
The Why of This Tale

Today, we shared a marvellous teaching tale based upon what Lord Yeshua has taught in every prior universe. Thus, the name of our teaching tale is **God's Greatest Miracle: A Tale of Two Little Angels.**

It is a tale about ***the power of perfected human love and hope***: a story about one little boy-angel and one little girl-angel born in Heaven.

Teaching spirituality to children and adults is more sophisticated than simple nursery rhymes, myths, fables, fantasies, and fairy tales. The latter creations are for pleasure or socialisation.

Even though teaching tales must use one of these narrative forms as a vehicle to inculcate sacred knowledge, these tales carry indispensable messages about our relationships with the Divine. Teaching tales communicate to the listener or reader information, telling us how God wants us to behave to fulfil God's Plan for humanity. The most ancient forms of teaching tales are myths and fairy tales.

But to teach spirituality, the storyteller must know the proper spiritual system to set the story within. In our case, such a setting was given to us by Lord Yeshua when he secretly transmitted this love story to Miriam of Magdala and his Beloved Disciple for safekeeping. So the proper setting is within the original and unadulterated Teachings Lord Yeshua gave during his Mission.

Therefore, the best genre title for this eternal tale of unconditional love is a Christian (spiritual) fairy tale. Why? Because the love shown by Lord Yeshua is understood best when told as a tender scriptural fairy tale. This tale can be recast in the settings of other spiritual systems for Unconditional Love is supreme. There is but One Law: Love is the only Law, Love under Wisdom. Love thy God and thy neighbour more than thyself.

Spiritual fairy tales implant spiritual knowledge within the novel's action, which seekers can experience if they desire. If you think about it, you see that our daily lives are stories and narratives. Our lives are like a kaleidoscope, full of pleasant and unpleasant events, events continually changing in front of us.

We have our heroes and heroines, helpers and opposers, our necessary and unnecessary suffering, and so on. When you sleep or use your creative imagination, the happenings of your day-to-day life work together to produce dream stories and adventures.

Spiritual fairy tales make for powerful sermons as the spirit of the community comes into resonance with the Holy Spirit. God's Greatest Miracle is presented in a format straightforwardly cast into three consecutive homilies. The Epilogue is optional.

I imagine it can be adapted for a children's play for Easter or Christmas.

Sacred knowledge helps us decipher our universe's global purpose and teaches us how to support this purpose locally. By paying attention to our thoughts, feelings, and actions, we come to see how earthly evolution prepared our animal side to serve Nature as conditioned biological machines.

Living machines, we remain until we understand we are more than just mere material creations. Associated with the physical device is an Essence-seed or angelic being. Our angels within may sleep, but we can ask them to awaken and guide our actions. When this happens, our minds enter a state of union with the angel within. The angelic vehicle becomes conscious and fully present in our life.

After that, our relationship with our daily life improves and stabilises, regardless of what is happening. We become Masters and Mistresses of our lives rather than helpless victims. Our mortal ego, the Me, connects with the angel within, the true I, whose home is the Kingdom of Heaven Within.

All you do is listen to the sweet voice within. It will guide you to the Hidden Door.

Knock, asking, "Open, I am lost, in despair, and have no one to guide me. Please help me. Open the door and hold me in your ever-loving arms."

If you are sincere and knock many times, the Hidden Door opens.

The living angel within says, "Come, child, never be alone again. I am your guide and Comforter. So you have nothing more to fear, for I will never abandon you. For you and I are growing together, so to be as one."

Never forget that the angel within is of Heaven. And Heaven is of Creator-Absolute. So, an ever-present conduit of love and wisdom for all sentient creatures is present, waiting for discovery and use.

With its hardships and challenges, the purpose of human life is for the angel to evolve consciously using sequential physical vehicles. But unfortunately, one physical body does not live long enough to complete conscious evolution. So, being transient, our bodies and minds need attention and care, not worship, for they do not exist after mortal death.

The purpose of learning and using sacred knowledge is to awaken from our natural dormancy and reactivity. When we awaken, we are conscious of the actuality of the moment. We perceive the bare facts without embellishment or degradation because of our biased, mainly inaccurate beliefs, opinions, and unwholesome needs and wants. Subsequently, no longer are we slaves to our conditioned, natural desires, but have become children of God.

Teaching tales allow the reader or listener to approach and begin living with the God of their Heart and Realisation, not the imaginary deity of theological speculation.

Like all real fairy tales, our teaching tale is very ancient. Storytellers told this tale to children living upon planets like earth in different solar systems and galaxies in many universes.

This tale came into my family during the reign of Catherine the Great of Russia. My distant forefather, Prince Aleksandr Mikhailovich Rurik, heard this tale from a dying Orthodox pope from Mt. Athos following the Battle of Chesme against the Ottoman Empire.

The pope explained. Christ told this story to his Beloved Disciple and Miriam of Magdala. They passed the tale down to others until it came into the hands of the dying pope's family. Pope Lazarus begged the Prince to memorise the story and keep it alive in the world. This Teaching came from the Father, entering Yeshua when the Holy Spirit descended at the River Jordan.

What could Aleksandr do, but make a death bed promise to the dying Storyteller that he would pass it down in his family? Thus, we have kept this teaching tale safe for over 250 years.

Aleksandr's scriptural manuscript included a handwritten note asking our family to share the old pope's tale with the world. Furthermore, the letter said to release it one century after the fall of the Russian Empire. Therefore, I must honour my ancestor's request.

I know some children and adults with spiritual ears, pure hearts, and honourable intentions will recognise the truths in this beautiful tale. They will find and teach others ***that Perfected Human Love is the most potent force for goodness in our entire universe?***

Every universe has Suns and planets like our earth. Each day, without fail, our sun shines down upon the surface of our brown-green-blue planet, providing light and warmth, giving life to all living creatures equally.

Without illumination by the sun, life wouldn't exist on earth. Therefore, as a solar system's sun is an absolute necessity for life, some storytellers call their sun Sun-Absolute. An apt name, in my understanding.

Does not our sun make you think of your mum or dad, brother or sister, grandmother or grandfather, aunt or uncle, or anyone who loves you very much? Who puts you into bed each night, tucking in your covers and kissing you softly goodnight?

God, the Creator-Absolute, has created Universes, planets, and little boys and little girls forever. There has never been a time when Creator-Absolute was not present. Always, Creator-Absolute is consciously observing, intending, knowing, and caring for all the Essence personalities living in the vast universe, whether within Heaven or Earth.

After the Creator-Absolute manifests a new universe, how it grows and fades away, having served its intended purpose, is beyond our tale's scope.

Tens of thousands of years ago, humanity learned to speak, and stories appeared. Entertaining stories about great heroes and heroines, great battles between good and evil, gods and goddesses, myths, fairy tales, and so on. Most of these stories were created by people wanting to share what they discovered in life.

Some stories come into the physical universe as dreams in which mythical creatures, ancestors, and deities speak to the dreamer, telling them an extraordinary story.

In the olden days and in underdeveloped parts of our Earth today, wandering storytellers visit small villages to share their tales. The storyteller usually arrives at midday and shares whatever news he has of the world outside. Then, as the sun sets, the villagers share a communal meal with the storyteller. After everyone eats, the storyteller is ready to start their tale.

The adults and the children gathering in front of the storyteller, excited about hearing another fairy tale, myth, teaching tale, or adventure.

Every storyteller must choose a child with a splendid memory and begin teaching them the story. After the storyteller finds such a child, the child travels everywhere with the storyteller. This way, the tale lives in storytelling families for thousands of years. Now, we can write any story we hear and accurately preserve one version of the oral tale.

Many people stopped listening to these stories after cities, civilisations, writing, and advanced technologies appeared. Sometimes, the storytellers cannot find children to teach. They would rather play games, attend parties, or watch sporting events. When storytellers die without passing on a story, we lose these incredible stories forever.

Occasionally, a story is so vital to humanity's future that the Masters refuse to entrust it to the whims and vagaries of everyday storytellers.

Teaching tales are gifts from Divine Masters, such as Yeshua, Buddha, Mohammed, Yogananda, and Krishna. Masters incarnating on earth so to save humankind from its Shadow or Darkside. Each Master introduces one or more teaching tales into the world, helping humanity overcome its dire predicament. Today, our world is dark, full of ignorance and evil.

The story we tell today is one of these teaching tales. Our tale is so vital that its guardians make sure that the message of the story remains unchanged. These tales remain, even after an old Universe passes away, returning to its Null State. Long after, human beings no longer exist.

I wish that you, the reader, will allow this tale to open the door to the Kingdom of Heaven Within, moving your centre of being from Earth to Nouseum. Then, together, we can overcome human evil and become the species God sees for us, *Homo dei* (as taught in the Eastern Churches). But only if we will wear our spiritual armour and fight.

About the Author

I am a real baron and a natural person who never stops exploring the boundless. I have had a rich life working as a medical doctor, research scientist, therapist, coach, author, lecturer, and spiritual mentor, all done to forward the Holy Family's plan.

I share this story with those who love and want to help God.

When I was three years old, I lived in Puerto Rico with a small band of courageous nuns. Their mission was to help unmarried young ladies abandoned by their families. The sisters told me that the families said their daughters were harlots and damned.

Sister Agnes Louise, my adopted granny, taught me the holy Family abandons no one, especially young, unmarried, pregnant young ladies. She taught me if you genuinely love Holy Mother, you do your best to love everyone, pleasant or not. And never forget to be kind to yourself, for Holy Father believes in you and knows you can do even better. Sister Agnes Louise's teachings formed the core of my being and guided my behaviour, though I have messed up many times.

Before I met the sisters, including the young noviciate I lived with for three years, Anna-Marie, I died in my sleep (I was born with a heart condition). I found myself in Heaven awaiting judgment. But Holy Father judges anyone. People just picked the place that they loved most to spend eternity. Good people end up in Heaven and bad ones in Hell.

To make a long story short, I asked Holy Father if I could be his helper when I grew up. Holy Father thought this was a grand request and sent me back to my bed, alive and healed.

So, I have done my best to be a good helper to the Holy Family in many areas of life. I know I fail at being what the Family wants me to be, but I don't berate myself, and I will do better next time. When you remember God loves you, things are just different.

This little book is about unconditional love, the love that Lord Yeshua showed all of us during his mission. I can't really love like Lord Yeshua. Still, I understand such love is a goal for all of us, regardless of our spirituality. I pray that this little teaching tale will resonate deep within your innermost heart. Hence, you feel the never-ending love of the Holy Family and how much they suffer for our oppressed, disadvantaged, beaten-down, and hopeless brothers and sisters.

Please, offer your heart and arms to the Holy Family as a helper on Earth, and maybe one day, we will make Earth as it is in Heaven. May the God of your heart and realisation become sovereign, so you find the keys to the Kingdom of Heaven Within.

Contacting the Author

If you enjoyed this book, please tell your friends and community about it. A short review of a few sentences would be grand on Amazon and Facebook if you really liked it. The more, the merrier.

You can locate us at jmpolyakovbooks.com, Facebook, and other social platforms under Jean-Michel Polyakov.

Ebooks, paperbacks, and hard-copies are available from Amazon, Indigo, Barnes & Noble, Book Depository and other platforms. Ebooks are available from our website. An audio book may be available later.

Jean-Michel can be contacted at email@jmpolyakov.com.

CPSIA information can be obtained
at www.ICGtesting.com
Printed in the USA
LVHW050334130422
716078LV00017B/383/J

9 780228 856894